THIS WALKER BOOK BELONGS TO:

_____

_____

_____

_____

For Amelia, Audrey and
Brooklyn the Chicken

First published 1998 by Walker Books Ltd
87 Vauxhall Walk, London SE11 5HJ

This edition published 1999

10 9 8 7 6 5 4 3 2 1

© 1998 Sue Heap

This book has been typeset in Opti Bevis Bold.

Printed in Hong Kong

British Library Cataloguing in Publication Data
A catalogue record for this book is
available from the British Library.

ISBN 0·7445·6330·5

Cowboy BABY

SUE HEAP

WALKER BOOKS
AND SUBSIDIARIES
LONDON · BOSTON · SYDNEY

It was getting late and Sheriff Pa said, "Cowboy Baby, time for bed."

But Cowboy Baby wouldn't go to bed, not without Texas Ted and Denver Dog and Hank the Horse.

"Off you go and find them," said Sheriff Pa. "Bring them safely home."

Cowboy Baby put on his hat and his boots, and he set off on the trail of Texas Ted, Denver Dog and Hank the Horse.

He went down the
dusty path and through
the barnyard gate.
Over by the hen-house
he found . . .

Texas Ted.
"Howdy, Texas Ted," said Cowboy Baby.

Cowboy Baby and Texas Ted
crossed the rickety bridge.
Down by the old wagon
wheel they found . . .

Denver Dog.

"Howdy, Denver Dog," said Cowboy Baby.

Cowboy Baby, Texas Ted and
Denver Dog crawled through
the long grass and out into
the big, wide desert.

There by the little
rock they found . . .

Hank the Horse.

"Howdy, Hank the Horse," said Cowboy Baby.

"I'VE FOUND THEM,"
Cowboy Baby shouted to Sheriff Pa.

"That's dandy," Sheriff Pa called back.
"Bring them home now,
safe and sound."

Cowboy Baby and his gang
sat down on the little rock.
None of them wanted
to go home.

"Let's hide!" said
Cowboy Baby.

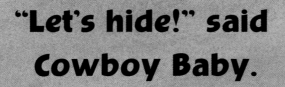

"Hey, Sheriff Pa," he shouted,
"I bet you can't find us,
            NO SIRREE!"

Sheriff Pa came to the big,
wide desert.
"Shh!" said Cowboy Baby
to his gang.

Sheriff Pa looked.

He looked . . .

and he looked . . .

and he looked.

But he couldn't find
Cowboy Baby.
No sirree!
"You got me beat,
Cowboy Baby,"
called Sheriff Pa.

"But if you come
out, there'll be
a big surprise,
just for you!"

Out jumped Cowboy Baby.
"Howdy, Sheriff Pa!"

The sheriff
threw his lasso.
It twisted and
turned in the
starlit sky,
and it caught . . .

a twinkling
star.

"Look!" said Sheriff Pa,
and he gave the
star to Cowboy Baby.
"Now you're my
deputy," he said.

Then Cowboy Baby picked up Texas Ted

and Denver Dog

and Hank the Horse,

and Sheriff Pa picked
up Cowboy Baby.
And all together they
went home . . .

to bed.

"Nighty night,
Cowboy Baby,"
said Sheriff Pa.

But Cowboy Baby
was already fast
asleep.

YES SIRREE!

MORE WALKER PAPERBACKS
For You to Enjoy

MOUSE PARTY
by Alan Durant/Sue Heap

A cat with a mat, a giraffe with a bath, a hen with a pen…
Mouse invites some very wacky guests to his house-warming party.
But then an elephant arrives and claims the house is his! A simple rhyming text and
illustrations full of humorous detail make this a great picture book for young children.

"Readers will want to rave on with this one until they drop." *The Observer*

0-7445-4390-8   £4.50

LITTLE CHICKEN CHICKEN
by David Martin/Sue Heap

Everyone laughs at Little Chicken Chicken when she makes a tightrope out
of a piece of string and says her black stones fell out of a thundercloud.
But when lightning flashes and thunder shakes the ground,
Little Chicken Chicken's magic goes down a storm!

"Dare to be different is the message of this uplifting tale about
the triumph of the imagination." *The Independent*

0-7445-5236-2   £4.99

MY MUM AND DAD MAKE ME LAUGH
by Nick Sharratt

Mum loves spots, Dad loves stripes, but their son has an
elephantine obsession that tops them all!

"Delightful for its brightness and consistency of concept." *The Sunday Times*

0-7445-4307-X   £4.99

Walker Paperbacks are available from most booksellers, or by post from B.B.C.S., P.O. Box 941, Hull, North Humberside HU1 3YQ
24 hour telephone credit card line 01482 224626

To order, send: Title, author, ISBN number and price for each book ordered, your full name and address,
cheque or postal order payable to BBCS for the total amount and allow the following for postage and packing:
UK and BFPO: £1.00 for the first book, and 50p for each additional book to a maximum of £3.50.
Overseas and Eire: £2.00 for the first book, £1.00 for the second and 50p for each additional book.

Prices and availability are subject to change without notice.